OPEN WOUNDS

Dixie, Washington, USA

© 2009 by Dixie Press
All rights reserved.

ISBN 978-0-557-23410-3
LCCN 8062559

Printed in the United States of America.

Preface

This is a work of love from members of the Lost Word Writers Group and me. My fans, and you know who you are, have been asking me to write a book of horror poetry for some time now, and since I finally freed up the time, I didn't want to do it without including my fellow writers in it.
Recently, my brother Leonard was married and I wrote a special poem for the occasion. I would like to share that here:

Sacred Vows

His

I can see a new horizon in your eyes
as I drink deeply into them and I realize
you complete me.

Your soul stays close
as your heart warms my own
the whole time I knew, I prayed
the perfect one would find me

Open wounds

Just make a wish,
I will make it come true
Just tell what I can do for you

Let our tears wash away our histories
so we can start our lives out new
Like a fresh rain in the springtime

Her

All I want to do is hold him
For he is the life, breathing in me
making me whole
he completes me

I want us to stay forever
always loving each other
souls embracing
Love un-ending

He wants to be a provider
as his family grows in numbers
and it love

She wants to be an open heart
not to replace a mothers love
but to be there when the love
is needed.

God believes in their love
and they believe in each other
two rings, one heart
a family that is the soul

Thanks and enjoy the nightmares!!

Acknowledgements

First thing I would like to do is thank the Lost Word Writers group for everything. I also need to thank my fellow contributers Devlin Giroux, Autumn Rose Wood, Cynthia Parker and Johnathin Nightthorn. Of course I need to thank friends and family and especially YOU! I couldn't write if you didn't read me!

Contents

I	DEVLIN GIROUX	1
II	JOHNATHIN NIGHTTHORN	3
III	AUTUMN ROSE WOOD	14
IV	TG REAPER	18
V	CYNTHIA PARKER	47
VI	FLASH FICTION BY TGREAPER	52

1

DEVLIN GIROUX

Circle

Does it hurt
when I put this gun
to your head?

Would it feel better
if I pulled
the trigger?

End it?

For us both.
We won't feel a thing.

Nothing new, this lack.

Open Wounds

Is it disturbing
how casually
I speak of our death?

This is not
something I want.
It only makes
the job
so much easier.

I could unload
set an empty gun aside.
Just relax and think . . . but…

Would lead me back to this.

2

JOHNATHIN NIGHTTHORN

Heart Beat

Throbbing, a slow, hard throbbing, like a bell

Inside my head, loud, so very loud, deafening

Softer underneath, a voice, I can't make it out

Words sometimes, but never sentences, pounding too loud

Can't make clear, strain to listen, yearning

Whispering, answers, demands, questions, whose voice

Yours, mine, whose voice, make the pounding stop

Stop it, stop, stop, stop, echoed by the throbbing

Open Wounds

Now not a bell, but that word, mocking me

Stop, no, stop, please, stop, don't, stop, stop

And still, behind, the whisper, so tempting, venomous

Then silence, then laughter, wicked, evil, taunting

Silence again, whisper comes clear, like a velvet razor

Licking me, cutting me, vile words, debilitating, crippling

The throbbing, please, come back, was wrong, return

Too late, gone, lost to the voice, in my head

Killing, logic, reason, gone, torn asunder, whispers

Whispers unabating, can't you hear it, tormenting me?

No more, no longer, stop now, please, can't, no, stop.

Open Wounds

No Game Unplayed

Do you feel drawn to me?

A fly to my great flame

To consume flesh and mind

Burn upon the flame of my wickedness

Is that what you want?

To lose yourself in the void of my heart

A great sleeping demon in the night

Or do you just want to touch the darkness

To feel superior morality by default

Ride the razor edge of destruction

Then retreat back to your healthy life

Do you think you can leave whole

Untainted by the darkness

It doesn't work that way

What I touch I change

Open Wounds

Alter to fit the soul

So come touch and play

But remember I am not a toy

I will be a tear in your reality

So come and play in the eternity of night child

And learn what it means to fear the dark

Open Wounds

Savior

The centuries slide

And I watch

Less movable than the mountains

More patient then death

Drinking from the river of humanity

I bide my time

My name becomes

Gyrating pale faces in clubs

I am courted from afar

A deviant god for the discontented

Throne of solitude

Love blossoms in absence

Eyes of stars I perceive

Open Wounds

The rise of the machine

Death of the collective soul

All is ready

The world burns

Pestilence spreads her hand

The starving masses feast on disappear

And I am moved

It is time to come forth by day

It is time to leave my legacy

Open Wounds

Digging Bones

My hands are filthy

Covered in dust and mud and blood

Grasping after long forgotten shards

As my nails break I increase my pace

Throwing handfuls with grim determination

Sifting threw the dead with reckless abandon

All to find that one damned lost piece of forgotten

Piles of desecration at my back like disturbed souls

Day by day without stop earth moves pushed by demented passions

No bottom to the pile, just one long tunnel of brown, black, and yellow

Just one bone

Open Wounds

Cyanide Dreams

Every night I kill you

Each time more violent, more visceral then the last

Your blood drips over me in hot red torrents

I play like a joyful child in your intestines

Carving patterns in your skin, an artist with the perfect medium

I lift you in my arms and dance you across the floor

With fish hooks I hang you from the ceiling, like drying a flower

I slit your throat wide and pour wine in your mouth

I lick the ruby fluids from your pale breasts, my special chalice

Then I wake, sweaty in my bed

At first excited, aroused, then disgusted with myself, but less each day

I shower and dress with you on my mind, threw all the day

When I see you I smile, remembering our night together

Open Wounds

You smile back, and I know, I just know, you dreamt of it to

I find myself wanting to reach out and touch you, sometimes I start to

But I wait, wanting it to be perfect for you, my love

I protect you from others, keeping you safe, keeping you pure

And each day I ask that one question, that all important question

Is today the day?

Open Wounds

Good Morning

Are you aware of the way your veins pulsate?

A steady rhythm, echoing the beating of your heart

It makes it very hard to concentrate

Your steady rhythm, seems to be tearing me apart

How devious of you to get to me this way

You just keep sitting there smiling, hurting me

That steady rhythm, visible on the back of your hand

Do you think I don't know, I know, I hear, I see

Damn steady rhythm, seems louder, getting distracted, and

And you keep getting, was thinking, louder, concentration

No, can't remember, wait, a hammer, gotta hit

New steady rhythm, I'm louder, who's the one who's tricky

Who's laughing now, I am, me, ha ha, that's it

Open Wounds

Nice steady rhythm, this is better, hmmm sticky

You were right momma, silence is golden.

3

AUTUMN ROSE WOOD

Parasite Poetry

Bleeding onto the page
All that rage

Trapped in veins
Letting the leeches drink and smiling while watching those bugs wither and die
Light with relief
Now that the toxins
Bloat tiny little bodies
Seeing the truth and feeling no pain
The poison released
Now that the lines are properly laid
Don't think about the cost
Someone else will pay, carrying the burdens
Just rejoice in the selfish freedom

Open Wounds

Bloodletting

Her disease is of the mind
Haunted by the clicking time
Her veins sliced by the sharp images
She see behind her eyes
Monsters – wearing the skins and faces of men – violate her flesh
Mocking her cruelly as a penis then a hand then a hammer
Mark her, enter her, and tear her
Is it memory or imagination?
Is it truth or is it recrimination?
Is it worth the agony?
She wishes for leeches to suck the poison from her blood
She'd be relieved to let the bugs drain her
She doubts she has much left

My demons never know when to quit
Making me write the lines that make no sense
Marveling at my stupidity and inferiority
I hate the lesions of time scarring my mind
I yearn to forget the lies I've told myself
I wish away reality until all I have before me is a blank page
Silence is my friend
Solitude is never my enemy
Searching inside for answers that can only be found outside

He is the doctor
He knows best
He wants to release the illness at its source

Open Wounds

Purge the putrid
Plunge deep into the veins
Plasmas dripping into the street

King of the Zombies

Zombies don't mock him, they seize him, but haven't a lot to say
Those strong reflects save him
He'll never be their meal, so he might as well become their leader
He wants to be king of something
His crutches slow him down, but he is still faster than a group of reanimated corpses
He'll not let them bite him to death or recruit him to their ranks
He will rule over them, an army that is really just a killing machine
He will march them to Washington, unleashing them upon the world, after assigning strict orders
Eat the idiots first!

Evil Bequests

Sinner visits the saint and asks a favor
Offensive Supplicant doesn't take kindly to denial
After the door closes the endowment appear
Slime in a hand basket
Decapitated cat in her purse
Blood stain handprint on the back of her skirt
Pussy footing around
Arriving with freshly killed birds and ripped open mice

Open Wounds

Nice little curse dropped on the porch
Answer the request before the earth is scorched
Malignancy isn't known for its patience

<u>Sunshine</u>

Smiles, bright, hide the hurt
Gaping wounds and bleeding hearts
Never see the light of day
Do not fear the darkness
That keeps two-faced evil away.

TG REAPER

FORGOTTEN MAIDEN, HE RETURNS
TGREAPER2003

Tears kiss her pillow
every night
loneliness has been a
faithful roommate since
he left

Trust and faith has long
since moved out
her soft heart, now
hard and brittle
a victim of his love

Her slumber welcomes
back the nightmare
his arriving home
another woman on his arm

Through half open eyes
she sees his corpse
sitting in the corner
and is relieved.
That nightmare is over.

THE WET SPOT
TGREAPER2002

It drips from the
ceiling.
Constantly,
raining bloody
teardrops.

Samantha died here
years ago.
Yet
The house still
weeps for
her.

Open Wounds

HAUNTED EYES
TGREAPER2002

I see through his eyes
Just before he kills
them.

I saw the blonde in the
pink sweater trip on carpeted
steps
hands over her eyes as the
knife found her throat.

The red head, a silhouette
in the shower
Curtain rips open
exposes flesh
crimson water fills
the drain.

I look at you as I say
this.

I look at you and see
myself.

I am the next to go.

Open Wounds

MISTRESS OF TORMENT
TGREAPER2003

She laughs at my pain
the snapping of bones
a melody of romance
in her ears

Green eyes dance
across bound wrists
as surgical steel
slides inside wet
forearms
My screams
the song of black roses

Her good times are the hardest
I pray for survival
another knife enters
final burial looms near
Her soul is wicked
yet I dare not save her.

Open Wounds

CHAOS
TGREAPER2002

I
am
insane
my mind
not
fractured
but badly
bent
The voices
in my
head
argue
and confuse
me
I no longer
know
who is
the evil
twin
Me?
or my
frosted side?

Open Wounds

RESIDENT EVIL
TGREAPER2002

I sit,
huddled in the corner of
this basement, as
Hell's minions storm the
house.

hairy spider legs,
enormous creatures
crawl the walls
searching the darkened
hallways for food.

Scientific upheavel,
experiment gone bad.
The living is now the
living dead. And I
will walk among
them.

Open Wounds

CURSE OF THE POET
TGREAPER2002

I stand cursed
throughout time.
Everything I say
comes out rhyme!

Now I wait to be beheaded
all because I said something
later regretted.

The king announced his wife
was dead
I followed it up with
too bad Fred!

I tried to say it was
all in fun
He had his guard
pierce my lungs

Now I sit, can barely
breath
waiting for the axeman
to come get me

GOOD-BYE
TGREAPER2002

I feel can feel you watch
me
Your hand touches my
shoulder when I cry.

Arms embrace me
when I miss you in the
night.

I know we'll meet again
in heaven

Until then, keep me warm
with your smile.
Till later, never
good-bye.

Open Wounds

DARK ROOMS OF THE PALACE
TGREAPER2002

A crash of thunder
shakes the building
Her head reels
tries to make sense
of things

Slowly, cautiously
makes her way down the
long empty corridor.

An evil presence is
closing in
She can feel it
Like a cold ball of fear
deep in her stomach

A heavy door closes
traps her inside
Red glowing eyes
greet her from
the darkness

Words on the wall
written in blood
"There is no escape"
She reads as white
daggers drink her
flesh

FATAL ATTRACTION
TGREAPER2002

Eternal bliss
hearts entwine
memories shared
throughout two
lifetimes.

His fingers, whisper
light, probe her curves.

"I'll always love you,"
He says before plunging
the carving knife deep
into her breasts.

Open Wounds

TAP
TGREAPER2002

Tapping noises on her
window.
tap, tap

She tries to sleep
but something
watches her from
the darkness.
tap, tap

Floors creep
and groan under
invisible feet
tap, tap

The door bulges
something large
is pushing from
the other side
tap, tap

Whispers
all around
her
tap, tap

A bony hand reaches
out of darkness
tap, tap

Her small voice
cries out
is lost in the
night

Tapping stops.
Silence
not even crickets
can be heard.

Open Wounds

THE BLACK MARKET
TGREAPER2002

She can barely
sign for the package.
Jitters rising. Pays and
runs to her room.

Slams bedroom door,
jumps on bed, knocking
over stuffed friends.

Shreds package. Sudden
disappointment floods her
veins. She ordered human hearts,
not livers. Liver gives her gas.

TASTY MRS. ROBINSON
TGREAPER2002

He pours gravy over
tender steak. Adds
corn and potatoes
for a finishing touch.

takes a piece and chews
slowly, savoring every bit
of flavor. Stops at a distinct
taste.

Mrs. Robinson must've been
a heavy drinker.

SHE WHO WALKS THE NIGHT
TGREAPER2002

She walks, stalking me.
I see her in nightmares,
she hides in the dark
corners of my mind.

She hungers. My blood,
my very soul, she desires.
Creation of the night,
she draws near.

I feel her icy breath
on my neck, her
ivory daggers pierce
soft flesh. I try
to wake up and
realize I wasn't
asleep.
I have been found.

Open Wounds

DARK PRINCESS
TGREAPER2002

She rises, eternally
young. Lusting for
fresh crimson nectar.

Empty heart, cold dead
stare. Shredding souls
without remorse.

She now darkens
my doorway. Lips
bleeding, my love
has come home.

Open Wounds

SONGS OF THE NIGHT
2002 TGREAPER

She listens to the night, even
as he rolls over, exhausted,
yet grateful for the trip to
paradise she allowed him.

Tiny fingers glide across
her breasts as thoughts
and memories and
sensations rain down her
body, holding her prisoner
in ectasy.

The night calls her. Wolves
howl in the distance, somewhere
a frog chants, reminding
her to stay within her
nature.

She drinks him slowly,
allowing his warm red nectar
to drip down her cheek.

His spent body twitches
in the moonlight, tempting
her to drink again. She
decides to answer the night.
After all, death leaves a bit
of herself as she passes
through the room.

MIDNIGHT GODDESS
TGREAPER2002

Lurking in shadow, blood
streaming down crimson
cheeks. White gown,
now crusted red, flowing
off slender hips.

He sees her cross the street
and knows he is doomed.
Body tight, eyes locked
to a demonic stare.

Fangs stretching, she
bites deep, a human
wolf shredding soft throat
into bloody scrap.

Thirst quenched, she
leaves the twitching
heap and rejoins
the night.

CURSE OF THE BLOOD
TGREAPER2002

He returns home at
dawn, physically
exhausted and mentally
drained.

He wishes he could end
it all, but knows the hunt
will continue.

Tears forming, Dracula
closes his eyes.

Open Wounds

EVIL WHISPERS
TGREAPER2002

You watch him closely.
Whispers of evil float
like ships in the harbor.

Glance in your rear view mirror.
Is that a dagger in his
hand?

You pull your cab
down an alley,
stopping at the
far end.

Door opens
he runs.
you glide over
the car's roof,
bring him to the
ground.

you feel razors
rip through soft
gums as you
impale his neck.
You drink untill
the twitching
stops.

Evil is in the
air tonight.
The hunt is on.

Open Wounds

BLOOD AT MIDNIGHT
TGREAPER2002

Moonlight seeps into
my room. Shadows
dance.
window opens.

Soft gentle breeze

He is here.

I feel his eyes
burning the darkness
His breath, hot on my
throat. Clock chimes
midnight.
He feeds.

A ROSE IN HER HAIR
TGREAPER2003

I only saw her for a
fleeting minute
a brief flash in the
journey of life

Her eyes, i don't
remember the color
but they were alluring
her hair, raven with
a rose, like a buoy in a
dark ocean, resting on one
side

I saw her delicate hands reach
for the man next to her
touching him erotically
I wished for that to be me

I saw incisors peek out from
soft red lips, and saw the blood
spray as she imbedded them
into his pale neck

Then I ran. That fleeting moment
is one I will never forget.
I only hope, that she forgets
me.

Open Wounds

DARK AS THE MOON
TGREAPER2004

I stand at her grave site
I see the earth move
before I cast my eyes skyward
to drink in the Gothic moon

Wolves cry in the distance
they feel her resurrection
As I feel the coming death

a struck match
glows in her vampire eyes
those beautiful, empty eyes

sulfur bleeds away, only the dark
separate us now
I pray to see morning

The moon glints off her ivory razors
a bleeding smile greets my throat
as I offer it to her

My lifeless body lies at her grave site
screams will be heard tonight
but these lips will remain as silent
as the October moon

Open Wounds

Vampire night
tgreaper2004

The eulogy rolls off a holy tongue
and falls on deaf ears
My dead heart will beat again
bloodless skin gleams in the empty moonlight
ivory razors peek out from wet red lips
my red hot thirst, so alluring
Whispers of bat wings
red droplets sprinkle her pillow
as she is taken by the night
I return to my empty coffin
my tomb, my prison until the moon returns
to release me

THE LEECH
TGREAPER2002

Red nectar seeps from
flesh tinted fangs
A human parasite
searches the night
for food.

He stands behind her.
She checks her reflection
while his remains shrouded by
his dark soul.
He feeds again.

Blood pours freely to the
dry thirsty earth
screams ignored by
empty streets. Body
drained, he searches.

Open Wounds

THE COFFIN
TGREAPER2003

Midnight calls for me
Fangs protrude
cut my lips
the taste enticing

I slam my fist into
wood, prepare
to join the darkness

Damn, door stuck
again!

Open Wounds

SUSPENSE
TGREAPER2002

Heart racing
Amanda saw the
shadow appear
outside the
window.

Something scratches
against the door
tries to get in.

Quietly, she runs to
the kitchen
Frantically dials the
phone
"please help me,"
she whispers to a
busy signal.

A window explodes
Footsteps crunch
against broken
glass, coming
closer.

Amanda ducks
under the sink
The footsteps get
closer. She crouches
down in her hiding
spot, hoping against
hope she won't
be seen.

A hand finds hair
and yanks her
back.

Breaks free
runs out of the
house and into
the night.

Open Wounds

Branches in the
woods cut her
hands and face,
but she doesn't
care.

She listens to the hum
of a chainsaw closing in.

As her screams fade into
the night, she knows she'll
never be heard from
again.

WEREWOLF
TGREAPER2002

Sunlight burns my eyes
as I crawl to my feet.
I can still smell the blood—
not my own. I grab a towel
off the couch to hide
my nakedness.

T.V. on, I hear of the
family ravaged by
wild animals as
memories filter back.

Tears of disgust fall
as I grab the pistol
off the table and
swallow the barrel.

Fingers twitching, I
slowly remove it, courage
fading. I pray for it to
return before the next
full moon.

Open Wounds

ISLE OF THE DEAD
TGREAPER2003

Welcome
to my eternal home
away from home
Your safe here
warm and dry
wrapped in the blanket
of darkness

My island paradise
is always just a
death away.

PUMPKIN HEAD
TGREAPER2002

Rifle loaded, blood streaming
down my nose. I hear it's
death screams from the
cornfields. It's returning
for me.

Screams closing in, I
trip on the spleen that
was once my dog.

Purple flesh fills the
window. I fire, blood
burning my eyes.

A shriek fills the

Open Wounds

room. Through crimson eyes
I see a flash of a bloody
talon.

It is the last thing I
will ever see.

5

CYNTHIA PARKER

Baby Cyclops

by Cindy Parker

under the covers
it squawks

in your ear.
it is a queer sound.

but no one's
around.

you think you might cry
when you see a third eye

glaring at you
lifeless. old

and cold.
you try to blink it away.
it screeches

Open Wounds

and wails.
but it's not

frail. it is inside
where it hides.

it only comes out
when you're in doubt

or about
to wake

up under the covers
when it smothers

its mother.

House of Secrets

by Cindy Parker

you made your home

in me.
but my walls are bleeding

gray.
the real you

i know. i see the mask
you leave with and discard

returning. it is i you cannot
escape. they tell me.

the blood of little shadows
cry to me. they tell me

everything.   i know

        all

your secrets.

Open Wounds

In One Form or Another

by Cindy Parker

i go. the way of all
mortals. the ground

waits. without thirst. patient.
indifferent. it simply

receives. just as it gives.
and gives back

what it receives. in one
form or another. all 613

bones
of me. i will awake.

to light. or to darkness.
whole

or broken. alive
or dead. in one form

or another.
if you don't know where i'm

Open Wounds

growing, be careful
where you step. or i may

just snatch you away
and take you with me where

i go.
in one form

or another.

6

TGReaper

WHERE EVIL LIVES
TGREAPER2009

    Nothing seemed out of the ordinary when I first woke up. I showered, dressed, and made breakfast all in the usual fashion. I sat down at the table and opened the newspaper. Suddenly I wasn't hungry anymore.
    I felt the memories slash at my dry throat like a razorblade, hungry for flesh. The demon that was my father stared up at me from the front page of the citizen patriot, his smile, hiding the beast that lived in his disgusting soul. The headline above him read LIFE TIME ACHIEVEMENT AWARD RECIPICENT. I read the article through tears of hate. Words kept creeping up, like outstanding citizen, giving person, loving family man. I wanted to scream at newspaper, blast it for its lies and deception, but the paper only printed what it was told to print. Toward the end of the article something really caught my eye. It read that my Father was now volunteering at the children's center. That beast, among hundreds of mentally ill children? Talk about a kid in a candy store.

Open Wounds

Childhood memories burned into my mind. Watching Father Pick up runaways on his mail route and bringing them home, only to chain them in the basement and rape them when the urges came back. Eventually the kids would either starve to death, or be beaten to death by Father wielding the same shovel he would use to bury them out behind the barn. That old farm is like a makeshift cemetery, the ground laced with human fertilizer. Mother, who I found out as a child was also my aunt, protected me from Father. My brother Bobby wasn't spared though, and whenever Father got the urge and there wasn't anyone else to quench it, Bobby would get a visit in the middle of the night. I used to cry myself to sleep listening to him scream and beg for mercy. We finally ran away at age 12 and 13 respectively. That didn't stop Father though; he still had his mail route. I looked back at the newspaper. All those kids…No. No more.

There were only two things my Father truly loved: sex and alcohol, and he didn't care where either came from. All I had to do was offer him both. Bait for the beast. I choked back a tear and opened the phone book.

"Hello?" His voice was damp venom.
"Father." I was fighting to stay composed. My greeting was met by silence and I couldn't help but picture him masturbating to the sound of my voice. Another childhood memory I thought was dead.
"Margaret? What do you want?"
"I miss you too," I replied.
"Sorry, but last I knew you didn't like me too much."
"I don't like you? You're the one who would never touch me." I wanted to vomit so badly. Total silence on the line.
"Did I lose you?"
"You…wanted me to?" I could hear the anticipation pouring into his voice.
"I didn't think you loved me," I lied.

Open Wounds

"It was your damn mother!" He snapped, thinking he missed out on my paradise. You're talking about yours sister, I thought, but kept it to myself.

"Well, she's not stopping you now," I said, trying to sound sexy.

"Are you serious?" He was really getting excited.

"I'll ride you like a horse," I said, then added "You've never had anything this good before." Now I was sure he was masturbating.

"Why all the attention all of a sudden?" His voice was barely a whisper. I had him hooked.

"I saw you in the paper, and it got me kind of bothered," I replied.

"Maybe we should get together."

"I have a bottle of Jack Daniels waiting for you. Drinks and paradise. Get here. NOW!"

I hung up as he was saying that he was on his way.

I had to move fast. I ran to the kitchen and got my sleeping pills out of the cupboard. I broke some into powder and dumped it into a large tumbler. Then I filled it with Jack Daniels and stirred it until the residue dissolved. Once it was finished I put it into the fridge to keep it cool. Then I ran to the bedroom and changed into my black nylon teddy. I was admiring my slender build in the mirror when I heard the knock at the door.

I could smell the dollar store cologne through the wood. He looked almost pathetic, dirty clothes, sweat pouring from the rim of his black hair down through his sweat soaked tee shirt. His eyes danced across my body, so I stood exposed, letting him take it all in. I felt violated just by him looking at me.

"Come in," I said, swaying across the living room. I could feel him watching my ass and I felt violated again, even though that was the reason I put the outfit on in the first place. I heard him drop in the recliner behind me. I was hoping to get him over to the couch so I could really work my magic on him. I got to the kitchen doorway and turned around, filling it up with my body. His eyes were getting plenty of exercise moving up and down, looking everyplace but my eyes. The thought of this pervert being my Father made me sick all over again.

"Be right back, Daddy." I batted my fake lashes and watched him melt all over my chair. Then I ducked inside the kitchen.

I came back a minute later, our drinks in hand. I swayed over to his chair, handing him his drink before sitting on his lap. I rubbed myself on his manhood and felt him shutter beneath me. He started to speak and I put my finger against his lips.

"Drink," I whispered. He took it down in one gulp, then started kissing my neck. I let him have his way with me until he couldn't stop yawning. Then I stood up and walked over to the couch. I had placed a roll of plastic behind it earlier when I started preparing for my beast of a father. I unrolled onto the carpet in front of the couch and patted it.

"Over here, Daddy. I don't want to get anything on my furniture."

Dad practically tripped himself staggering over to me. He laid down on his back and stared up at me with an evil grin on his face.

"I'm going to make you my regular Saturday night thing baby girl," he slurred.

"Thank you," I whispered, straddling him. He looked up at me in anticipation as I slowly lowered myself down onto his stomach. By now he was weak as a kitten and barely able to keep his eyes open.

"You've grown up nice," he hissed, trying to stay conscious. I moved up until I was sitting on his chest, my shins pinning his arms to the floor. I could feel his lungs fighting for air beneath me. Too easy. I reached up and pulled one of the couch pillows and put it firmly on his face. I stretched out and laid across it to make sure I had enough pressure to do the job. I stayed on the pillow for a solid five minutes after his fingers stopped twitching, just to be sure. I knew Bobby would be coming soon so I ran to the pantry and pulled out the hack saw. It took nearly an hour to dismember the bastard and put him into garbage bags, and another hour to clean up the mess and toss the remains in the

Open Wounds

dumpster outside. I had just enough time to shower and change before he got there. I was glad Bobby was coming over. The whole encounter made me feel rather horny, and my brother was the best I ever had. I was going to have to marry that boy someday.

7

TGReaper

THE VAMPIRE/ZOMBIE WAR
TGREAPER 2009

I could barely see the wet ground in all the rolling fog. Moonlight washed the graveyard in pointed shadows. I stood among the dead, powdered resurrection in my hands. I sprinkled the chemical mix throughout the Potter's Field section, choosing cadavers that no one would ever miss. From that area I could see the Parlor estate, where Vlad Parlor was no doubt watching me prepare for his nightmarish attack. The estate appeared one night in the fall; it had been a field before that. No one ever saw the construction of the place, it was just there. Soon afterwards animals were found with puncture marks on them. The townsfolk started blaming the chubricabra, the infamous goat sucker. But that was just ridiculous. No such thing. The truth was, the war was coming. Vlad was raising his army of vampires, I was raising an army of the dead, and the city would be ground zero. A pack of wolves sang off in the distance, his children of the night. Then I remembered. My God. Tamisa was back at the lab, and Igor was alone with her.

Open Wounds

I could hear her slamming into the cage as I entered the building. I ran straight to the lab, which was at the far end of the dark hallway. Igor was standing in the doorway, loading the tranquilizer rifle. He saw it and tossed it to me just as Tamisa slammed into the cage again, this time breaking the gate open. She landed on all four, her nose sticking up in the air, no doubt trying to smell our blood. She looked beautiful in her wolf form, standing under the moonlight, just below the lab window. I took aim, closed my eyes and squeezed the trigger.

The dart slammed into her side, sending her smashing against the wall. She fell to the floor in a heap, already turning back to her human form. I covered her up and had Igor take her to another cell. She begged me to help her, and I had every intention of doing so, but first, I had to rid the world of Vlad.

The next day was spent loading my guns with special bullets, empty shells filled with holy water and wolfs bane. I had some vampire blood saved up from one of my many kills, and I had Igor rub it under Tamisa's nose. I wanted my best weapon ready for battle. I knew I was just using her, but she could forgive me later. Sunlight was ending quickly and my army still hadn't come down from the hill where Potter's field was kept. I started to worry that I didn't use enough powder.

Moonlight was just starting to wash the land when I heard his voice.

"Human! Come out here and face me. How dare you attack my minions!" Vlad's voice was dripping with anger. I grabbed my rifles and instructed Igor to go fetch Tamisa. I was going to need all the help I could get. I draped my neck with my crucifix and started towards the back door. I peeked through the window on my way out. The parking lot was filled with vampires, with Vlad standing at the center. I didn't have enough ammo to take so many out. I checked my weapons, including my handgun that was full of silver bullets, just in case, took a deep breath, and then stepped through the door and into the night air.

The vampires were poised, ready to pounce. I aimed my rifle at Vlad, who grinned.

Open Wounds

"Human. My shields would never let a single bullet touch me. Why not surrender yourself now and allow my children to feed?"

"I'm no one's dinner, Count!" My voice gave away my fear. The army of vampires slowly closed in, stalking me from all sides. I was going to die tonight. My powder didn't work, and Igor was taking his sweet time with Tamisa. By the time he would get here it would be way too late. I closed my eyes and waited, I always thought I would go out with guns blazing, but right now it seemed so useless.

"Protect me my children!" Vlad screamed out from behind the wall of vampires. I opened my eyes and saw them all turning, facing the army of zombies that were charging from the hill. Better late than never. I ran back to the door just as it burst open. Tamisa charging out in full wolf form. She liked the smell of vampire blood and wanted more. Igor limped out behind her, grinning ear to ear.

"Fantastic, Igor!" I said.

"Thank you Master," he replied.

"Igor, you can call me Doctor Van Stein."

"Docktor Van Swine. Yes master." Igor had the worst time trying to pronounce my name. We've had this conversation before. He would start calling me anything that sounded remotely close to my name, until I would give up and tell him to call me master. For some reason, going through the name slaughter again sounded like a pain in the ass.

"Igor, call me master," I sighed.

"Yes Master," he replied, and then added under his breath "Narcissist bastard."

He never was very good at whispering.

The zombies were being swarmed. Several vampires were biting down on them at all areas of the body, then, in turn, would burn up into ashes. The holy water I added to the powder mix was running through their veins, and the re animated hearts were pumping it throughout the bodies. Vlad watched in horror as his army burned away in front of him. He must have been really dis-

Open Wounds

tracted because he didn't see the blood soaked werewolf until she slashed his throat with her paws. His eyes bulged as he looked at Tamisa in disbelief. Pedicure in holy water really did the trick. She slashed him again, taking the head off of his body.

Just like that, the war was over. Two zombies were left, and Tamisa made short work out of them. I pulled my handgun out and aimed it at her. She looked at me with demonic eyes, her curse demanding my life as well. She charged as I emptied my gun into her. The impact sent her backwards through the air. She landed among the burn marks in the parking lot.

"I'm sorry Tamisa, this is the only cure I know of," I said, staring into her lifeless human eyes. Igor had already started picking up the zombie parts and piling them into a cart. He would cremate them later in the basement's boiler room. I instructed him to cremate Tamisa as well. He acknowledged me then called me more names under his breath. I would have to replace him soon; he was really starting to try my patience. But first thing's first, and I had a cadaver waiting under a sheet in the lab. While in the cemetery I found a fresh grave that had a usable brain in it. It used to belong to a serial killer, but since he was executed, he wouldn't need it now. The weather channel had predicted a thunderstorm tomorrow night with plenty of lightning. If my experiment worked, and I could recreate life…real life, not the temporary zombie stunt I pulled, the medical world would finally take me seriously. Frankenstein would live again.

TGReaper

THE ROAD OF LOST SOULS
TGREAPER 2009

"Are you sure we're going the right way?" Brenda asked for the third time. Her brother rolled his eyes, which she noticed.
"I don't want to nag, but you know what they say about the area."
"Bull shit," Keith replied. "No such things as ghosts."
"I don't know," Brenda continued. "I've heard things."
Keith slowed down his Beetle and turned down a dark gravel road. The moonlight created eerie shadows along both sides of the Volkswagen. He didn't reply to his sister's ranting, just stared straight ahead.
"Especially the kids from Morning side. They say that the kids come out on the anniversary of the fire, looking for souls."
"Who are they?" Keith asked.
"You know, they."
"I know that they are full of it, and I can prove it."
"How?" Brenda folder her arms across her chest.

Open Wounds

"Easy. Tonight is the anniversary, Morning side is right over there, and they're no kids…" Keith's voice trailed off. He brought the car to a full stop, not taking his eyes off the road.

"Keith?" Brenda shook her brother, who pointed out the windshield. Brenda turned and looked into the eyes of a dozen kids standing in the headlight beams. A young girl walked to the front of the pack, right up to the hood of the car. She pointed a finger at Keith and the car shut off. Lightning filled the skies and a wind came out of nowhere. Brenda looked from child to child, their expressions sending chills down her spine. They were all staring, with hate and death in their eyes. A young boy stepped forward, and like the girl, pointed at the car. The Volkswagen began to shake violently as if it was in an earthquake. Two other girls walked to either side of the car, pressing their faces to the windows.

"You are going to die tonight," they chanted. The other children joined in.

"Oh my God!" Brenda said, covering her eyes. Keith, calm as always, eased himself down in his seat.

"I wonder if anyone will find our bodies," he said.

Martha Shuberg was scared senseless. She knew the stories about Morning side, but this was the only way back to the highway. She cursed herself for not starting before nightfall. She rounded the curb just in time to see two adults being led by the hands by a group of small children. They seemed to vanish as soon as they left the road, leaving a Volkswagen beetle with its headlights still trained on the night. Martha knew what she saw, deep down, she knew she just seen the spirits of Morning side. She knew, but she left anyway. It was easier to deal with a guilty conscience, than it was to deal with the dead.

9

TGReaper

THE OPEN SEA

TGREAPER2009

    Commander Zurich checked his watch for the fourth time. The tour boat was over forty five minutes late, which for Captain Frank Smith, was unheard of. It was a quick trip around the "Haunted Islands", then back up the coast line where the cruise ship would be waiting. The local islanders protested, citing that the islands were cursed, which made the trip even more exciting for the passengers.
    "Ship ahoy!" one of the ship mates announced. Zurich stared through dusty binoculars as the away boat turned from the island and towards the awaiting S.S OPEN SEA. He felt a very brief wave of relief wash over him, before the chill returned. Something was terribly wrong. He ordered the crew dockside to help and called the ship's doctor and put him on full alert.
    Ten minutes later Zurich was sitting at the desk waiting for Dr. Roberts to return. When he did, he had a very concerned look on his face.

Open Wounds

"Sir, we have a serious situation here. The boat left with the captain and seven passengers. One is missing, six are dead, and the Captain has absolutely no memory of what happened."

"Damn." Zurich rubbed his chin, trying to filter through everything that was just dropped on him. There were dead passengers; families will have to be notified. There was also a missing passenger, so a rescue team would have to be sent. His head was ready to split.

"Do you know anything? I mean, what killed them?"

"Well, they all had markings on them, almost like burns on their arms. Even the Captain. But from what I could determine, and this was without any autopsies, their bodies just gave up. Like something wore them out."

Zurich leaned back, staring up at the ceiling. "Do you have anything for a massive headache?"

"Sure do," Dr. Roberts said, reaching for the lower drawer on the desk. "I think we both need a double."

Two whiskeys later Zurich sent two of his best crewmen out to search the islands for the missing passenger. He stood at the ship's wheel, pondering what to do next. Finally, he decided it was time for help.

"Com, call the Island authorities, apprise them of what happened and ask for assistance." He listened as his officer relayed the message. Within minutes he had an answer.

"Commander, they are ordering us away from the islands immediately."

"What the hell?" Not without our missing passenger and crewmates."

The com officer was looking at Zurich while listening to his earpiece. "Sir, they say it's for our own protection."

"Protection? From what?"

"From me…" The voice was like a whisper chewing glass. Zurich turned back to the wheel and stood face to face with the missing passenger. At least, what used to be the passenger. His

Open Wounds

lips were peeled back in an insidious smile, his eyes, jet black, no white showing anywhere stared deep into Zurich's soul.

"What the hell?" Zurich said again without realizing. The creature held up a finger and shook it in front of him as if scolding him for swearing. Zurich could see smoke pouring from the creature's arms.

"We are not your plaything," the creature said, his large mouth barely moving. "We are to be left alone. We tire of your curiosity."

"Who the hell are we?" Zurich asked, standing his ground like a good sailor. The room suddenly filled with the smell of wet fish and what reminded Zurich of the meat department of Wal-Mart. He knew in an instant that he was surrounded. Nervously, he looked around and saw the crew and remaining passengers standing in unison. The deck outside was also filled with them, all staring with evil smiles and black eyes. The doctor and the captain were among them as well.

"Look, give me back my crew and we'll get out of your hair."

"They are we now, and you will be an example."

Hundreds of hands tore at Zurich, he pulled away, but his arm remained, tearing off at the shoulder. He screamed as his other appendages were torn away, leaving him on the floor. The creatures dropped down, chewing away on his organs, smiling the whole time. He closed his eyes and waited to die.

An hour later the rescue boat returned to find the S.S. OPEN SEA missing, with a sign in its place that read WE DON'T WANT YOU HERE. Commander Zurich's half chewed arms were attached to the sign, which was connected to a pole coming out of the sea. The crewmen looked at each other, and then turned the boat to the open sea. Neither said a word. Nor were they ever heard from again.

10

TGReaper

JACKSON BURG
TGREAPER2009

    Travis pulled up underneath the only working streetlight on the strip. The general store stood like the rest of the town, empty and dark. It was like a ghost town, everything were it should be, except there wasn't anybody anyplace. Donna moaned softly in her sleep. Travis looked down at his young wife. Blood was starting to seep through the wet bandages on her arm. He reached down and ran his fingers through her soft brown hair. He had to do something.
    Travis pulled the car up a little farther, just out of the light, and then climbed out and into the pounding rain. He crouched by the front door of the store, looking for any alarm system. In doing so, his hands slightly pushed, and the door opened without a sound. He took one last look around, his eyes falling on his Buick and the precious woman bleeding inside it, and then he went inside.
    The first thing he noticed was the security cameras. They were propped in each corner, each having the wires unplugged

and dangling in the shadows. A wave of relief poured over Travis. He wasn't a thief, and if the store was open, he would pay for everything. He found a first aid kit in the middle of aisle four, next to the can goods and engine oil. He grabbed two handfuls of cupcakes from the hostess display and carried his goods up to the register. He reached over and pulled a plastic bag from behind the counter and dumped everything into it. Then he slipped back to the door, and after checking again for any onlookers, he slid back out into the wet night.

Donna was starting to stir as Travis pulled into the hotel. It was a three story box, generic, and yet comforting at the same time. Travis looked down at Donna, who was studying her wet bandages.

"How are you feeling?" He asked.

"Like I fell from grace."

"Well, more like fell on your ass, but I won't get technical," Travis said. "C'mon, let's get you inside and patched up."

Travis half walked, half carried Donna into the hotel. Like everyplace else, the reception desk was empty, and all the keys were neatly arranged on the board. Travis looked around to make sure the coast is clear, and then grabbed a set of keys.

"Looks like were in fourteen b," Travis said, studying the keychain.

Two hours later Travis was sitting in a recliner staring out the window at the night sky. Donna was sleeping on the bed, her wound freshly dressed. Travis was about to fall asleep himself when the bathroom light turned on. He looked over at Donna, who stirred softly, then returned to whatever dream was making her smile. He walked over to the bathroom and slowly opened the door. The tub was filling with hot soapy water, and two candles were lit at the far end.

"What the hell?" Travis whispered.

"For me? You're so sweet!" Donna brushed past Travis and started searching for a towel. There was a set of them neatly folded in the cabinet. Travis took another look around before closing the door. He didn't want to tell Donna that he had noth-

Open Wounds

ing to do with the candles or bath; he didn't want to scare her. He walked back over to the recliner and was soon snoring in it.

Something brushed past Travis's arm, waking him up. Moonlight was filling the dark room, casting shadows on the walls. Donna was on the bed, sound asleep. It didn't take long for Travis to realize he wasn't alone. He jumped out of the recliner and found himself surrounded by people. Men, women and children, in various uniforms and outfits. They wore blank expressions, just stared straight ahead.

"Are you comfortable?" A soft voice echoed from somewhere in the room.

"Yes, thank you," Travis said. "Sorry about the store. I needed bandages for Donna."

"She fell," The voice said.

"Yeah, we were camping, and there was a downpour. She slipped and rolled down a hill. There was some barb wire in the foliage and she wrapped up in it."

"She will be fine," the voice said. "Rest."

"Travis wake up!" Donna's voice brought him off the chair in an instant. She was sitting in the dining room, her back to him. The smell of eggs and bacon filled the room. Travis walked over to Donna, who was reading a get well soon card. There were two plates loaded with steaming eggs, bacon, sausage links and toast. Travis sat down across from Donna and started eating. She looked up at him with shock in her eyes.

"What are you doing?" She asked. "I didn't make this; it was here when I woke up."

"I know," Travis replied. "I think I met the welcoming committee."

"What the hell is going on?"

As if in answer to Donna's question, there was a knock on the door. The couple exchanged looks before Travis slowly walked over to the door. He opened it to an empty hallway. On the floor was an old newspaper. Travis reached down to pick it up and suddenly felt dizzy. He shook it off and took the paper back to the table. Donna was eating heartedly when he returned. He sat down and read the headlines.

"Town poisoned by unknown source. Investigators looked into the possible disappearance of town's people when communication coming from Jackson burg suddenly ceased. Upon investigation, the residents were found dead, most of which were sat around the dining room table, breakfast still in front of them." The couple looked at the food, then each other. Eyes bulging, Donna tried to stand and fell on the floor. Travis tried to move, to help her up, but couldn't get his legs to move. He could hear the same voice from the night before.

"Welcome to the neighborhood."